MAN BEING

Volume IV: *Bucephalus*

MAN BEING

Volume IV: *Bucephalus*

Communicated to
Dramos & Bohemias

Front Cover Artwork by
Giovanni Domenico Tiepolo
"The Procession of the Trojan Horse in Troy"
Created in 1773

9 781999 177775

The following is a tale. These are The 7 Prophecies of Macedonian King Alexander the Great. This is the story of how Man Being overthrew its Rulers and re-opened the Gateway known as "Terra".

TABLE OF CONTENTS

Introduction

THE RETURN
OF ALEXANDER

| INTRODUCTION |

In the days before his disappearance, King Alexander, Liberator and Leader of the Macedonian Armies instructed his men to follow him into Hades:

"Our Kingdom extends beyond the winds of this world and into a realm brighter than seven of our Suns. Follow me good men of Macedonia and gallop beyond Asia Minor toward the Elysian Fields. For this war is a mere skirmish and this world a dim reflection of the Great War of our ancestors. Today your swords pierce the flesh of men, but tomorrow, the horns of demons."

Now, more than two thousand years have passed since Alexander's Silver Shields crossed the Hellespont into Persian territory. The Earth plane remains ravaged by corruption and atrocity. Alexander, from the Immortal realm, communicates a warning to Dramos and Bohemias. His prophecies are recorded in this text for the good of Mankind and so that the sons and daughters of all humanity can rise from the ashes of a world, soon left behind.

These
are the
Seven Prophecies of
King   Alexander   the   Great

REOPEN THE GATEWAY

| PROPHECY ONE |

1 This is a warning and an explanation. The Ruler of the Beings who are obstructing you and preventing you from leaving the confinement of Earth, is what we will be discussing. When you obtain the understanding of this message you will be activating an affront. This confrontation will be monumental. There will be a warring faction and epic activity that occurs globally. Please understand that the release of the gateway obstruction is causing damage and upheaval in the Earth plane. There is, on another level of experience, an ongoing war that many of us continue to be a part of.

2 There is gold and a fight for the resources in the 3rd density. Some of us have been sent to help release the obstruction to the gateway, and more will be returning to continue the work. The event of 2034 to 2060 is a linear time period where we will be directly involved with the activities in the Earth plane. This is an undertaking that is continuing and is heading toward a completion. This release in writing will release a signal that creates a monumental unity, but also a confrontation in the 6th density. This confrontation is reflected in the Earth plane experience, as what occurs in one level of light or dimension of experience is also experienced in the 3rd density. Earth plane is a reflection of an activity that is occurring in another level of experience. The warring that is occurring is also reflected in the activities, confrontations and misery in the Earth plane.

3 You will experience war and disease and many things imploding in the Earth plane. Your activities and experiences on your planet are a representation and reflection that mirror other activity occurring in another dimension of experience. The Inner Earth experience, Terra, is the gateway. The fight to release and open up this obstructed gateway is resulting in monumental fatigue of infrastructure and systems in the Earth plane. This will cause war and pestilence and the complete upheaval of the existence for Beings on the planet. The luminaries are shifting and there are global catastrophic experiences that are the forerunners of the implosion of civilization and all that has been created on the planet. You are heading into a disaster that has not been experienced since the flood.

4 You must unlock the mystery of the gateway. You must redefine the experience of The Disconnect, as in the "death experience". The events that lead up to a mass ascension event include the unlocking of the gateway and the instructions. You are revisiting again the same action and activity. We are attempting again to overthrow the obstructed gateway and require everyone to release their light and open up not only their individual ascension portals, but the gateway for the cosmos. Everyone must align their energy together for the event. The event of course is not a linear day, it is the ascension release as written about in your "Book of Revelation". The gateway is opening up. The luminaries are imploding. There is a massive upheaval on your planet. There are hidden gold resources. The physical location of this gold on the planet is a starting point for the mass ascension, which is culminating in the location of the United States of America.

5 There is an upheaval in earthquake and volcanic activity occurring in the United States of America. There is a physical understanding that the Shambhala existence occurs in the United States. The Ascension Event is the release of the obstruction of the gateway and the overthrow of the Rulership of the Draconian Beings. Please prepare as you are encountering Draconian energy. The Beings who are associating with the Repair project to reopen the gateway in the Earth plane will be identifying that they are interacting with these Beings. This is a warning. However tempting, do not interact with these Beings.

6 Please remember that your written accounts and your experiences in the Earth plane are a reflection of events that occur elsewhere and so the adage "as above so below" is an apt understanding and explanation. What is occurring in your linear histories is in fact a reflection and an account of a tale that is occurring elsewhere. The warnings and the tales and the dissemination attempts have occurred repeatedly. The language has changed and so the code has also changed. There has been repeated explanation and instruction for the Beings in the Earth plane and attempts to get the instruction to you. This is now being achieved. Why have there been so many changes in the language and why are there different languages associated with different physical areas on the Earth plane? You are speaking about information that has been recoded and changed. As the information about ascension and the attempts to release this information occurs, there is also a change in the language. Notice the recent changes in your English speaking language, particularly in the United States and the use of slang. There has been a dramatic change to the written and spoken language through the use of the short form via texting on your devices. The information is now being confused and the communication is becoming more difficult and rife with hidden interpretations and meaning.

7 The toppling of your English language is occurring. Language is imploding once again. You are no longer able to communicate with one another. Generation gaps are occurring but this is more than a younger generation with a "hipper" form of communication. This is the overthrow of your spoken and written language to completely confuse you. You are no longer communicating with each other. You are no longer able to communicate effectively with one another, as there is an intrusion of different meanings and interpretation of your words in your language. Soon, you will no longer have the resource of spoken and written language. This overthrow of language by what you call slang and short form communication is disrupting the exchange of code. This tale is occurring at a momentous point in the history of the language, particularly in North America. Specifically, this heralds the downfall of your civilization in the United States.

BUCEPHALUS
& THE TEAM

| PROPHECY TWO |

1 Pay attention to the tale of Bucephalus, the "companion Horse" of Macedonian King Alexander the Great. It is written that this was my horse. Bucephalus was not a real horse, but a myth created to disseminate information. Bucephalus spells out coordinates. These coordinates are the places that The Team occupied when they last executed the mission, but aborted. The Team is assembling again and will form a Star with each point on the eight-pointed star representing a coordinate. These coordinates will be revealed and the Team will be asked to place themselves in these points. The points are not spaces in between the light or places, as you might be imagining. These points are ways for the Team to connect with others in the network. The network is the interconnected paradigm shift or the new way that members are going to be speaking with each other and collecting other Beings for part of this mission. There are other Beings who are involved in this. The name Bucephalus represents the Beings that are involved.

2   The points of the Star, the Beings. You will understand that the Star they are forming is a way to open the gateway. The gateway opens when you have absorbed the meaning of this message. The Beings who are carrying the information and the understanding on how to coordinate is what you are now relying upon. There will be a gathering of the other Beings who are involved in executing this mission. This mission is not a new mission. We are recreating the previous attempt. Bucephalus will become clearer to you as it does not represent a physical horse or animal, as you have been led to believe. This analogy is simply an exercise to gather the Team together to work in a unified front. They will be entering a zone whereby they must connect and resemble something that they are not. In order to pass through the DRA energy field the Team must experience an existence that they have not yet remembered. The way to pass through is through invisibility and the invisibility requires the Team to simultaneously be in a synchronized experience. This is equal to the Trojan Horse tale described in the Iliad. This is what that tale was about. This tale is reoccurring and has always reoccurred. The specific details of the 2034-2060 event are described in the Iliad. Your readers can equate Helen with Terra. She has been abducted and obstructed by the DRA. There is also an understanding that I am directly affiliated with the "demi-god" Achilles, which is accurate although written about in a way that is condescending and not in a positive light. These "tales" have been staring you all in the face for centuries.

3   The Team members cannot be separated. They are not allowed to individually proceed. They have a commitment and an arrangement whereby they all are interfaced and are communicating in unison. The sound they are making is unlocking the gate. The key. They are making a key together. There is a Being who you are now being introduced to: Aurelius. This Being is not known in your historical writings or understandings. Do not confuse this Being with another Being of the same name.

4 Aurelius has the anatomy of a human with a lion-like or feline-like face. Aurelius' hair appears wild, although it is not hair as in human hair or hair as it would appear in the Earth plane. The hair on this Being is in fact light. The quality of this hair would pose a danger to human touch, as though being cut with a laser. The eyes are very close to human eyes in the way that they look but also in the way they function, although they are also able to absorb information the way that your mouths or noses do. The eyes communicate, as this Being does not make sound with its mouth. Aurelius is a leader in a faction, a group that previously abandoned the project and had gone off on their own. This is a renegade group.

5 You are not yet ready to enter the next world. We are gathering the other Beings. We are making a key with the union of these other Beings. The key is the frequency, something that happens to unlock a gateway that will allow us entry into another world, another experience. We will be sharing and communicating in a language of light. It will not be human language.

6 The Team. These Beings got stuck. The information and the mission cannot be retrieved without full completion. The mission cannot be abandoned without ramification. The Beings, Aurelius being one of them, were not able to translate the message in time. There is a mission and a message to free the Earth prisoners. They were not able to translate it. They were not able to decipher it. They didn't have someone who could decipher it for the Earth prisoners. Decipher does not mean "understand". We are saying that they needed someone to operate in your 3rd density Earth plane, someone who could have their feet in both worlds. It requires someone who can relay the message from the 3rd density. There is a repercussion once the message is received. It must be relayed immediately. In linear terms, "time is of the essence".

7   There are many that will insist these writings and symbols are fraudulent. That the information and the context is not in fact consistent with what has already been relayed in your religious texts. There are other Beings that have attempted to recreate or invent the existence of this information and organizations that have been created based on this incorrect and fraudulent activity. This message will undoubtedly cause many to lose their livelihood if a light is shone on the truth. The Team is presenting the correct information. The correction is what will upset many, as they have built their lives around its existence and their beliefs as such.

DECIPHER THE SYMBOLS

| PROPHECY THREE |

1 This is an instruction and an operation. The tools provided are an opportunity for an uprising from the Earth prison. This message has repeatedly been toyed with and repeatedly reinterpreted and confused for the masses. The message included in the bible texts is also something that you will be revisiting. The information and the instruction has been written about in many accounts and historical tales but truthfully nobody remembers what the story is about. The reality of our situation is that time as you know it, in the Earth plane imprisonment, is of the essence. You are no longer equipped with a repertoire or ability to handle the mass chaos and destruction that is headed your way.

2 We are speaking about the Earth and we are speaking about the Earth plane. Freedom from the imprisonment is not something that will be neat and tidy. We are speaking about war and warring factions. Instructions will be given and interpreted and relayed to those who are ready to receive the information. Please understand the following. You are being asked to publish and relay the information. You are Messengers. Please adhere to the responsibility. We are not asking you to do anything beyond publishing and making available the instructions. Those who are equipped to understand the instructions will be able to set forth and understand what their mission and responsibility is. What we are suggesting is those who are reawakened and understand the mission will step forth. This is not an exercise in "spreading the word". The message or instruction will be published and those who have the eyes to see will receive it.

3   You will not be receiving the information as in "a talk". This has dangerous implications and consequences if the information is recorded. You will be receiving the information in a combined effort, mostly through instruction following a dream. The dream is not what you are writing about but there is instruction in the dream. You will be receiving symbols. These symbols have been received before in this exact and precise order.

4 The instructions hold a map and a sequence and the sequence allows travel through a gateway and a stream, an energy stream. The instructions on how to get through the gateway have not been forgotten. They have been confused and they have been manipulated, repeatedly. Why are these instructions now waiting for both of you to publish and communicate? Why not have somebody else do this work? We have decided that your cooperation is appropriate. Many Beings through the ages have acquired this information and resorted to nefarious activity. This has been repeatedly and also rapidly exercised. In your historical text and accounts there are unusual stories about wars and populating new lands. These descriptions are actually pointing to the gateway exercise that we speak about. Do not be offended by the cryptic nature of this   talk.

5 We will present the information to you in a layered way that will drift through the dream state and will also be received in a vision form. This is not done to isolate or to interpret things as in someone's faculties are more accessible or stronger than another's. This is done to prevent the absconding of the information and tools. This is a very simple exercise. You will be releasing the book quickly without much fanfare. Do not worry about unlimited text and interpretation not being available for the masses. The interpretation is there for those who can receive it. You do not need to concern yourselves that the book seems short or seems incomplete. This is the exercise. Readers will be confused and also fascinated and this is a necessary step. Those who are meant to receive this information will learn about the book through others who do not know what to do with the material.

6 You will receive instruction on how to interpret the symbols. You will sketch the symbols. You will record the symbols. You will present a table of symbols. The table is in a classical sense in the way that it is organized. It will be what you are expecting it to be, as there is no other form that you can publish in a physical book in the Earth plane. The information itself is not the book. The book is already published in another reality. We are just retrieving the information. This book is sitting etherically in the Hall of Records. This is a retrieval. Why has the retrieval not been successful previously? The power that one may wield when they engage in this information is such that most derail and lose the focus. The original intent is lost.

7 There are power struggles. Being involved in a human paradigm and the Earth imprisonment state makes one long for physical immortality, an endless supply of riches and also the power and control of the Earth plane. Man Being is so easily corrupted and so easily believes that the task is to accumulate people and riches and power. This is how the governments are structured and the agencies that are holding the keys. This is the reason why you are all imprisoned in the belief that you must make a name for yourselves by continuing to control the imprisonment. Those that are controlling others are succeeding. Those that step away from the paradigm are martyrs and so on and so forth. This continues. You will not be corrupted by the power. We are aware that you have no interest in seeking the limelight in order to share this information and so we are preparing you for the communication.

8 There will be an explosion of information and other events that will continue through 2021 in government agencies throughout the world. There will be changes in the political structures.

9 You are both primed so you will understand what the experiences are. Symbols are energies and are also experiences. These are all one and the same. You will no longer relegate your experience to words written on the page. Symbols have a life of their own. Language is energy that has been trapped and trapped in this case on a page. You are now freeing the experience. You will be introducing something that has not been released in its proper communication or state. The symbols or letters have a life and activity of their own. They are able to write themselves. Symbols, energy symbols, light symbols. You are containing energy and light in the Earth plane and do not understand what you are doing when you speak. Most of you are not working with the light. You will soon understand what communication is.

THE 144, 000 SPEAK

| PROPHECY FOUR

Alexander refers us to a Group of Beings who wish to speak. They are the 144,000.

1 We are The Army spoken about in your Book of Revelation. They imprisoned us. They put us here. We combined efforts. We tried to stop the war. They've locked us here. They choose to put us here. We are in a comatose state but can communicate with you and other Beings while you are in the sleep state. They put us here after we arrived, thousands and more. We are retrieving the mission, the instruction. We are to contain the enemy forces. We are to restrain. We are to enable the force. We have been instructed on how to contain energy. The state of the energy is similar to what you are referring to as the jinn state. We exist in a state that is not equivalent to your state of being. We cannot control our desires or thoughts. They are manipulated by the Others.

2 Who are the Others? They are Draconian. They are here now and you will soon see that they can achieve the goal of controlling the human race by instilling a substitute for air. They are attacking the air. You will not be able to exist if you do not choose another way. There is a demonstration that is starting. This demonstration is tiered in a way that allows spectators to create a belief that they no longer adhere to. We are reminding you that you are continuing this mission. You will reveal their hiding place and where they are exiting from. You are revealing the exit points. The coordinates. The war has begun.

3 There is an entry point. You have learned about fields. You have learned about energy fields. You have learned about transmutation, portal belief and changing one's very existence. They are arriving to take over not only the planetary alignment but also the conditions for which we remain imprisoned. You will not be able to make your way to the gateway if we are not released. There are Beings who are waiting to act. You are part of this alignment. The reawakening is not about a spiritual reconnection with ideas that transform your thinking. We are speaking about your reemergence. You are sleeping and will be made whole and continue the work so that you can avenge the others.

THERE IS AN OPENING

| PROPHECY FIVE |

1 What is happening is the reawakening, not of your beliefs as these are certainly in place, but the awakening or the reawakening of others...there are other Beings. There are other Beings involved who have a stake in this situation. There is an undertaking. Your mission is to get word, which you have successfully achieved. You may not understand or see this as you cannot see and also be and also relay the information in the Earth plane. It seems you both do not remember why, and I am here to remind you both that you have already achieved the goal. You are repeating and re-executing a mission that has failed repeatedly. You do not understand why it has failed. Your understanding is not required. What is required is your full participation, which you have both agreed to. There is an understanding. There are other Beings involved here. The Beings we are speaking of are the 144, 000. The Army.

2 The 144,000 have communicated with you. The mission involves these Beings. There is a war that is occurring unbeknownst to many of you in the Earth plane who do not see or do not wish to see. Many of you have had questions about biblical explanations as in the books you are wondering about. Biblical books as in Revelation have often been perceived as a description of this exact situation. And although it is a correct understanding the undermining and the belief that this is a religious conquest and mission is simply incorrect. There is a battle that is underway because the gateway or Terra is in a hijacked state. Of this you are now both aware. Terra will be reopened.

3 There is in fact a physical gateway and opening. A "Messianic" experience will guide those who are ready to make their way through the gateway. The gateway that leads to the other galaxy is what you are writing about. Few will truly believe that this is underway. The earth plane pandemic has already been described in the biblical text and you are under attack again.

4   The question about disease is not in fact something that is affecting you biologically. This is in fact a greater ramification as this is affecting not only your immediate atmosphere, but also the other layers. This is in fact a change in the energy stream and the way the various layers are organized. We are speaking about the stratosphere and the layers above and below including the microbe layers that you are creating with this so-called disease. There is certainly more to your pandemic than has already been written about in various conspiracy theories and hypotheses. The damage to the air is what will be causing the chaos, not in fact the disease that you are focusing on. You are all focusing on the wrong problem and therefore you are distracted and not prepared for the onslaught.

5 There is an opening or a crack in the gateway that has been previously sealed and keeping you entrapped. Things are opening which may sound at first like a positive development but the Others, the Draconians, are making their way in. There is an antiquated belief about demons and the air and this is something that you will draw upon when trying to understand your "current" situation. The instructions and the coordinates will be released and The Team will reunite.

6 Those who do not wish to believe will not believe. Those who are waiting for this information will of course absorb it and perceive it in a very serious light. The parasitic Beings are also searching for this information. They do not have the access. They are waiting. Not everybody who receives the instruction is helpful to the undertaking. Once this is released, it is released and available for all.

THE AIR IS CHANGING

| PROPHECY SIX |

1 You are being punctured, appropriated. Your pandemic or your Virus is preparing you for the truth, but the truth is not about defining one's disease of physical being or the appropriate immune function or dysfunction. The disease is the air disease. Not as in the airborne transmission of pathogens that are destroying your physical wellbeing, but in fact the frequency of the planet or the planetary alignment is what is causing the problem. The Others, the Draconian Beings are able to enter a physical form and space that is occupied by another energy or Light Body. The invasive parasitic nature of these Beings of course you are both fully aware of, but what has not been written about is the project to release these Beings back into your very place and space of existence, in the realm you are calling Earth plane.

2 There is a belief that what you do not see does not exist and many of you still sadly subscribe to this misunderstanding. What is manifesting is now the creation of these Beings through the belief in the Virus or the Virus mandate. This is creating a situation that bears resemblance to a god and entity that you are collectively forming with your confused beliefs. You are allowing these Beings to reside in the Earth plane in other bodies of Beings who are already trapped in the Earth prison.

3 The collective consciousness of these Beings, the Others, are creating in fact a mandate, a god, an energy, a collective presence. The antiquated beliefs about the air or the wind quality must be reconsidered. These Beings have made many attempts to enter the Earth plane. In order to allow the gateway to open this is a necessary situation that unfortunately we have not been able to secure or correct. When the gateway opens, the opening allows all to enter and to also exit. You are regarding this situation as an exit strategy, as in making your way through the portal, the gateway, and escaping the Earth imprisonment. Remember, when the gateway is fully open, the entry and exit points remain and Beings may go in either direction. The reincarnation cycle is an example on a smaller scale of what can occur.

4 The permanent existence or coexistence with these Draconian Beings is an ongoing struggle that has occurred more than once, as your biblical texts are explaining. There have been floods. There have been disasters. The air, the airwaves, the destruction of the air is something that is a byproduct of the portal or gateway being forced open. The opening is not a lid or a doorway that one physically unlocks, you are creating it collectively with your misinformed beliefs about disease. You are creating an egregore.

5 The function of these prophecies and tales is not to explain to readers the dynamics of positive thinking and positive changes. The purpose is to share specific codes and coordinates that will assist them with the onslaught of the entry of these Beings into the Earth plane. You have only had glimpses of the trouble that you are all about to face.

6 The codes and information are not a magical grimoire that will allow you to escape unharmed. These are a systematic series of frequencies and therefore beliefs that will allow you to create an impenetrable form so that these Beings do not overtake you and coexist and ultimately destroy you. The destruction of your Light Body is of course a grave concern and not something to be taken lightly. If you ask, "how can light be destroyed", this is more the question that you can be focusing on. These Beings have the ability to destroy the light. These prophecies are effectively creating an armor that will allow readers and the other Beings that they associate with to protect themselves. You will notice that those Beings who do not subscribe to this belief stream are being effective in a very negative way, being overtaken by these Draconian Beings. The evil and the chaos in the Earth plane is about to increase at a new level unprecedented in all of your historical accounts of war.

7 For the majority of you the experience will be war and a warring faction. Some of you will be able to physically see and witness what these Beings look like and how they cohabitate with others in a shared form. The majority of you will experience great distress. You will soon see where the problems of war are created from.

8 You will see the function of the 144,000. These are Beings that you refer to as Angelic Beings. These are not of the Draconian origin. These are Beings who have been involved in battle before and will be involved in battle again. These are Beings that you are aligned with. You do not realize the ramifications and so you are slowly being led to the understanding. This understanding is necessary for you all to absorb. The understanding that there are other Beings who are being held captive and will also be released is a truth that is necessary to absorb.

9 It has begun. There is a war that is underway. The levels of which will reach a height in 13 years from this publication. You will see that the event and the ascension events coincide with the horrific Earth plane disaster.

PARASITIC UNIONS

| PROPHECY SEVEN |

1 The affliction and the air and the division of the air explain how the light or the Light Body may be executed or modified. There is a mandate by the Draconians to execute the Light Body take over. There is a danger of being enveloped or more exactly, smothered. These Draconian Beings are able to execute and fulfill a decision to overtake our Light Bodies. Our Light Bodies in our natural state of being are free from danger. The imprisoned state of your Light Bodies makes you all vulnerable to attack. The ability for these Beings to overtake your form is what you must concern yourselves with.

2 We are not equating this with fortifying your physical form as in protecting what you perceive as good health and good health state. The frequencies you are being exposed to now are making you vulnerable. Many of you have noticed your sensitivity to certain sounds and the increased awareness of background noise and background sound experiences. You are being penetrated or punctured, as has been described earlier, through frequency. The understanding that the air is being attacked is not an exact description but the understanding that the air is composed of Beings who you are now encountering directly is more or less what you must describe to your readers. These Beings are coexisting with you now, in closer proximity.

3 Some of you are aware of these Beings but are not affected. The rest of you are now in direct encounter. Those of you who are obligating yourselves to the Repair Project are in the most danger of being overtaken. Overtaken and no longer occupying your form, your Light Body is released and disconnected into the atmosphere and into the world of these Draconian Beings. Being ejected from your imprisonment in the form is not what we are asking you to achieve. You will feel as though you are exiting your form. This is not a desired outcome. If you are disconnecting you are disconnecting into the world of the DRA.

4 There are hybrids among you. There are also Beings who are in close contact and communication with Draconian entities, who have not yet been overtaken. Remember, it is the form that they require in order to disconnect from the Earth plane. They wish to penetrate and occupy the Earth plane. They wish to be released from their parallel existence. As we move toward the next World War, these Beings will be released and enter the Earth plane. You presently coexist in a parallel state. The Earth plane is not singular. There is a split. You are now being introduced to the split.

5 Please be aware that mandating or encouraging disconnect when your readers do not have the information on how to cross over or cross through and exit the Earth plane correctly, is a dangerous direction or instruction. You must clarify on the matter. What happens when you disconnect and you are not ready? This is how the DRA or Orion DRA state, the hybrid state exists. Those Beings who are disconnecting are also now being hybridized. This is not information that we want to be misconstrued or misunderstood. You must be clear on this. There are many hybridized Beings in the Earth plane who have begun their disconnect either through a direct action or have inadvertently been preyed upon. Those Beings who are unaware of the parallel state of existence in the Earth plane are vulnerable to the attack. The attack is not about your death. The attack is the attack of your physical form as in a break and enter situation. Being vulnerable does not equal inevitable doom. You are equipped with the knowledge now, and this is your armor.

6 When the exit attempt is made there is an experience whereby the Light Body may separate from these DRA Beings. If the attempt is not successful the Light Body is extinguished permanently.

7 The concept of "Hell" is being revisited as it has been misunderstood and incorrectly described. There is no Hell as in a place and space of eternal damnation, as has been described in your religious scriptures. There is a state of being however that is a permanent state, whereby you are permanently locked out of the portal. The portal being the accessed gateway (2034-2060) through which you must travel in order to shed these Beings. Parasitic cooperation exists in the Earth plane and is the reason of course for all the atrocities. These are concepts that you are fully aware of but do not regard as exact truth because of the way that they have been presented.

8   Hell as many of you refer to it, is a self-inflicted experience and not one of punishment for bad behaviour. It is an existence when one realizes that they are trapped and want to escape. It is the fear and desperate need to escape that will create this state. The need to escape is what must be worked with. There is a mandate and an instruction on how to avoid the destruction of the Light Body, but not by shoring up the physical form. It is in fact the frequency that must be blocked or changed. We are asking you all to begin the signal. It is the signal that you are creating to destroy the frequency that is making you vulnerable to the attack.

9 If you have formed the parasitic union you are still able to be reunited with your singular Light Body experience, but you must not create a split from these DRA Beings. You must allow these DRA Beings entry through the portal or gateway with you. This is the exact truth and one that is perhaps unfathomable. Beings who realize they have encountered evil or an evil state of being ultimately wish to exorcise themselves from the situation but once this state of being has begun there is no turning back. Unfortunately these parasitic Beings must cross with you in order for your Light Body Being to continue. This is what has been explained to you previously in other dialogues. You are not leaving these DRA Beings behind. There are very few of you in the Earth plane that exist without the coexistence of these DRA Beings with you.

10 The vast majority of you have been taken over by these DRA Beings, as in you are already in a hybridized state. There is now a heightened attack on the Beings who are bringing forth truth and assisting in the Repair Project. The Beings responsible for the Repair Project are not presently in hybridized state but are extremely vulnerable to attack.

11 Those of you bringing forth truth are swimming in a current of evil now. You are coexisting with these DRA Beings, but not in a formally hybridized state. You are swimming in the same medium as them. Many of you have already encountered these DRA Beings. You do not have to experience them in a vision or dream or a full on encounter. It is a general feeling that they are around you. It is the air you breathe that is now the problem. You are breathing these Beings. Be aware of the poison and the poisonous frequencies that you are being exposed to. Members of the repair project have been given tools. There is a frequency and a signal that you make and this is what is protecting you from the attack.

12   You are being given instruction in specific frequencies, a string of frequencies. A frequency or signal is not one sound. It is a composition of frequencies. A monumental sound. This has been recorded in the Book of Revelation.

13 The pandemic state has created an awareness that you are all too close for comfort. The need for the physical distance from exposure to the virus is the same thing as the need for the distance from the parasitic attack. This is an attack through the air. The airborne disease creates a hole in the wall that divides you and the other DRA Beings. They are waiting to destroy your light.

14   The belief that "all will be fixed" once you disconnect and release yourselves through the gateway is not entirely true. Many of you have formed a parasitic union with these DRA Beings. We are explaining that you must already accept your hybrid state and make your way through the gateway, albeit an arduous journey for most. The signal you are being asked to create is being deafened by the frequency that these DRA Beings create within you. You are being exposed to frequencies that are unhealthy and contributing to serious mental health problems in the Earth plane.

15 The signal that is being created by those Beings who are not compromised will assist everyone, whether or not they are able to strongly generate these healing signals or frequencies. It is the exposure to the new medium that will help and assist everybody in the ascension experience. Those of you who are repairing and partaking in the Repair mission are creating a new medium or a new signature. Please be aware that the atmosphere is changing. The Atlantis story is now being introduced. You are creating the experience. The flood is the signal.

16 There are many Beings on the Earth plane emitting this protective and healing signal. The number has been mentioned already. 144,000 is the correct number. You are reawakening the Army. The purpose of the Repair Project is to sound the trumpets and the next chapter will unfold on December 8th 2021.

INSTRUCTION

| THE SYMBOLS |

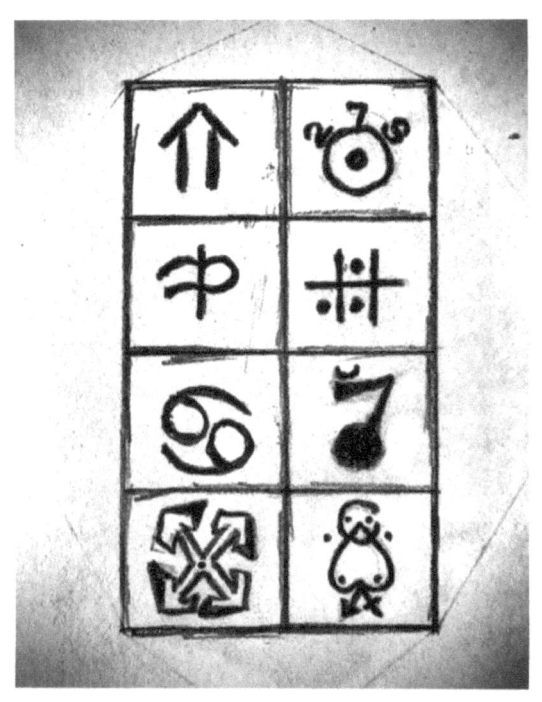